The

(Underappreciated)

Life

of

Humphrey Hawley

Written By

Mathieu Cailler

Illustrated By

Carrie Louise Wood
+ Rebecca Wood

Summary: "Humphrey" is about a beetle who wants to be a ladybug because he sees the way ladybugs are loved by humans; however, after time spent pretending to be something he's not, he learns to love his world and, more importantly, himself.

About Media Group
PO Box 667626
Houston, TX 77226
For information about custom editions, special sales, readings, signings, events corporate purchases, or donating copies, please contact About Editions.

For all the Humphreys out there.

"I used to think I was the strangest person in the world, but then I thought there are so many people in the world, there must be someone like me who feels bizarre and flawed in the same ways I do. I would imagine her, and imagine she must be out there thinking of me, too."

—*Frida Kahlo*

The

(Underappreciated)

Life

of

Humphrey Hawley

Humphrey Hawley lived in a tall pine tree with his mom, dad, and older brother, Dominic. He thought being a beetle was boring, and he'd often crawl to the far limb of his tree and take in the view of his park.

More than anything else, he wanted to be a ladybug. They were so glamorous and fun. And children seemed to love them, too. Humphrey always heard the boys and girls giggling whenever they found one, calling out, "Look! A ladybug! Wow!"

Humans didn't care for beetles. One time, Humphrey took a shortcut and crossed through the park's sandbox. There, he passed a little girl. He waved, but she screamed and rushed off to the swing set. Humphrey was devastated.

As Humphrey watched a group of children toss a Frisbee, his mom called out to him. She was making sap stew and needed him to collect twigs, dry bark, pine needles, and a few blades of grass.

Humphrey inched down his pine and scoured the lush lawn. "Hey, Mom? What do you think?" he heard a voice say.

Humphrey craned his neck and spotted a woman and boy, sitting on a nearby bench. Humphrey trembled with fear and excitement. *Humans!* he thought.

S o, what do you think?" the boy said again.

Humphrey knew he shouldn't linger, but he wanted to better see the family. Carefully, he crept to the table's surface to inspect the humans. His heart thumped in his chest and his fingers tingled as he gazed at the mother and son. They were painting the pine where Humphrey lived, their canvases swirled with thick globs of color.

Just then, a gust pummeled the park. Humphrey fell to the ground and shielded himself, tucking his head into his chest. When his antennae no longer thrashed in the angry wind, he opened his eyes.

The stiff breeze had taken the boy's cap. "Mom!" the boy yelped. "Mom! My hat!" The cap traveled fast, rolling like a tumbleweed. Both the mother and son jumped up and sprinted after the hat.

Humphrey took a deep breath and gathered himself. He scurried back up to the park's table and strolled around the brushes and dipped his hands in the gooey colors. An idea popped into his mind: *What if I painted myself to look like a ladybug? Would humans love me? Could I finally be proud?*

He spun around and located the boy and mother. They had retrieved the cap and were making their way back towards the bench.

Quickly, Humphrey shoved his hands in the red paint and smeared the sticky oil over his shell. It was hard for him to reach his lower back, so he flopped over and rolled directly in the bright guck. Then, he tossed up a few flecks of black paint and let them splat on his body.

Next to him rested a glass jar, and Humphrey savored his reflection. His abdomen, elytra, and thorax gleamed in the soft sun. Warmth buzzed about his body and his lips bent into a small smile. *I'm no longer a beetle! I'm special now!*

"Hey, look!" the boy said, now wearing his cap. "A ladybug!"

Humphrey grinned and his eyes grew wide. "You're right, sweetie," the mother said. "How beautiful those colors are! They almost look like paint!"

Humphrey took full advantage of his new look, strutting down the boy's arm, wrist, palm, and fingers. "This is so cool!" the boy said. Humphrey agreed.

The mother grabbed the little glass jar on the table. "Here, sweetheart," she said. "Why don't you take the ladybug home?"

Humphrey couldn't believe it. *Humans want to bring me home! I'll have a new life!* He fluttered his wings and wiggled his toes. The mother handed over the top of the container and Humphrey slid inside the jar, landed on his feet, and listened to the boy screw the lid on tightly.

It all happened fast, and now Humphrey was in the backseat of a car, heading down the road, staring at the boy's face through the thick glass container. "Can you put some rock music on, Mom?" the boy asked. A roar of sound rushed through the walls of the car. *Rock music is cool!* Humphrey thought.

Out the window, Humphrey's park grew smaller and smaller and, soon enough, the green field, strong trees, basketball courts, and sandbox vanished from sight.

They arrived at the humans' house. The boy set Humphrey on his desk and sliced a few slits into the jar's lid with a pair of scissors. "Hi, Ladybug. I'm Chuck," the boy said. "I'll be right back." When Chuck returned, he opened the jar and dropped in a few pieces of clover and a sharp twig.

Later that evening, Chuck's mother entered and got the boy ready for bed. She tucked him in, pulled the blanket all the way up to his neck, and kissed him on the forehead. "Where's your painting?" she asked. "Why don't you hang it up?" She located the picture of the tree and hung it above Chuck's desk. Humphrey pressed his face against the jar. *My park. My tree. My family.*

The next morning, Humphrey was awakened by a voice. "Good morning," Chuck said. He was so close to the jar that his breath fogged up the glass. "Today's a big day," he said. "You're coming to school with me. I have this presentation called show-and-tell where I have to bring something to class and talk about why it's cool. I bet no one is going to bring in a real ladybug!"

Humphrey couldn't believe it! *I'm going to be the star of show-and-tell!*

Soon after, Chuck's mother dropped them both off at school. "Be good," Chuck said as he stored Humphrey in his outdoor cubby. "Show-and-tell isn't till one, so I'll come get you then." Humphrey nodded. He thought about what he could do to entertain the class. *Some handstands? Some backflips? A little breakdancing?*

Humphrey waited in the hot cubby. He stared out the glass at wandering butterflies and buzzing bees. Even though he looked like a ladybug, he was still a beetle, and he missed wadding on fresh bark and tasting fresh air. He missed the way his mom would hang upside down and call herself "Bat Beetle," and he missed how his father would tuck splinters into his mouth and imitate Dracula. *It's really hard,* he thought. *It's really hard pretending to be someone else.*

The sun's rays beamed directly into the jar. At first, Humphrey had been able to handle the heat, but it was now unbearable. He fanned himself, flew up towards the slits, but it didn't do much good. He was *really* sweating. Little beads slithered over his face and back and legs and arms.

Chuck continued: "So, for show-and-tell, I decided to bring in my favorite insect, the ladybug!"

Light rushed into Humphrey's eyes as he left the security of Chuck's pocket and was plopped onto a small table. Humphrey rested his hands on his hips and stood strong, like a superhero.

The class erupted into a raucous laugh that seemingly shook the jar's glass and made Humphrey shudder. He gazed at all the children's open mouths. The laughs kept coming and coming, pouring and pouring.

"That's not a ladybug!" a little girl said. "That's just a beetle!" The students continued to chuckle and snicker. *What?* Humphrey thought. *How? Why?* He rotated his head and inspected his body. *The heat*, he remembered. *All that heat in the jar. All that sun made me sweat. And all that sweat made the paint melt off!*

Chuck shrugged. "But I—" Chuck started to say. "I don't—" Humphrey hung his head and whispered that he was sorry. He knew he'd disappointed the boy and all the other students.

The teacher clapped his hands a few times and the class fell silent. "Students," he said in a sharp voice. "Students, please. That's enough."

The teacher took the jar in his hands and lifted it up towards the ceiling. Humphrey felt all the children's stares burn into his shell.

"As you know, this is not a ladybug," the teacher said. Once again, the children tittered. "No, this is a beetle. One that is pretty common in these parts. We see them all the time on the field, in the trees, even by the jungle gym. But did you all know how special beetles are?"

Humphrey's eyes snapped open.

What? Me? Special?

"Really?" a student asked.

The teacher continued: "Oh, yes," he said. "I loved studying them in college. Boys and girls, did you know that there are over 300,000 species of beetles on the planet? Did you know that adult beetles wear a sort of body armor? Did you know that they have been on this planet for over 200 million years? And… did you know that some of them can even glow in the dark?"

With each interesting fact, Humphrey puffed out his chest. He blinked rapidly and stuck his hands back on his hips. He glanced at Chuck. The boy wore a huge smile on his rosy face.

Wow!" a student piped up. "So beetles are super cool?"

"Yeah," Chuck answered. "Beetles are awesome!"

"Sometimes we don't think of certain creatures or things as special because we see them a lot," the teacher said, "but they are. The air, the trees, and, of course, beetles. Why do you think a rock group decided to name themselves after this insect? Because they're amazing!"

Humphrey's limbs tingled. *A rock group named themselves after us? Whoa!*

A hearty ovation took hold of the classroom, and Humphrey scanned the students' faces, big and wide, smiling and nodding.

"Now, Chuck," the teacher said, "while I appreciate you bringing this incredible insect to our classroom for show-and-tell and allowing us to have this learning opportunity, we need to remember this is a creature that needs to be one with nature. So, boys and girls, follow me, please."

When the class reached the field, they passed around the jar and each child said good-bye. At last, the container found Chuck. "Good-bye, buddy," he said. "Thanks for being so cool at show-and-tell! Beetles rock!" Chuck ripped off the lid, and Humphrey shot out of the jar. He spun in the sky and whirled around the students. *Oohs* and *ahhs* escaped the children's mouths and joined Humphrey up high.

From the air, Humphrey pinpointed his park. It wasn't far away. He flapped his tiny wings and flew faster than ever before. *I'm a beetle*, he thought. *I'm a beetle!*

He landed at his park. It was more beautiful than he remembered. The sweet scent of pine washed over him as he trekked up his tree. "Mom! Dad! Dominic!" he let out.

"Humphrey!" they shouted.

They all rushed towards the center of a curved limb and embraced. "Sweetie!" Humphrey's mother said over and over. "Where have you been?" Father added. "Yeah, what happened to you, bro?" Dominic asked.

Humphrey didn't know what to say. He remained silent for a few seconds, looked down at the branch, and then said, "I got lost... I got very, very lost."

Mother, Father, and Dominic hugged Humphrey tightly. "Well," Mother said, "now you're very, very found."

Humphrey stayed still in their love. The weather was warm, the wind soft. And he didn't want to be anywhere else. "Hey, what's that I smell?" he finally said. "Is that what I think it is? Is that sap stew?"

The End

Acknowledgments

If you've made it here, I assume you've finished the book. And now, here you are, reading the acknowledgments, which is amazing (and a little strange). I never got into writing for anything other than to tell stories and make people happy. What I do doesn't save lives, but it can be a sort of "cookie" after a long day, and there's value in that, I think. I thank you for your time, and for reading, and for the ride we've just shared. It means a great deal to be held in your hands.

This book wouldn't be possible without the amazing Editor-in-Chief, dear friend, and all-around brilliant human, Anthony Ramirez. I thank you for your mission, your purpose, and your dedication to art.

To the illustrators, Carrie Louise Wood and Rebecca Wood: I thank you for giving Humphrey life, and this story power. Without you, his tale is simply a yarn in Times New Roman, size 12. Nothing more. You gave him soul. I'm ever so lucky to have worked with you both.

To the students I've had the pleasure of teaching—I thank you. I taught you math; you taught me everything that mattered.

To my family—you always stoke my fire, even when it's down to twinkling embers.

To Lou, my sweet dog—thank you for hanging out with me in various coffee shops, on my desk, and in hotels.

Deepest gratitude to my friends (in no particular order): Racquel Henry, Christiana Metzenbaum, Maggie Morris, Tim Antonides, Kali VanBaale, Donald Quist, Kevin Grosher, Sophfronia Scott, Cheryl Wright-Watkins, Amanda Silva, Jennifer Cohen, Courtney Ford, Christina Gustin, Catherine Buni, and Susan Solomon.

About the Author

Mathieu Cailler's poetry and prose have been widely featured in numerous national and international publications, including the *Los Angeles Times* and *The Saturday Evening Post*. A graduate of the Vermont College of Fine Arts, he is the recipient of a Short Story America Prize for Short Fiction and a Shakespeare Award for Poetry. He is the author of *Clotheslines* (Red Bird Press), *Shhh* (ELJ Publications), and *Loss Angeles* (Short Story America Press), which has been honored by the Hollywood, New York, London, Paris, Best Book, and International Book Awards. His most recent collection of poetry from About Editions, *May I Have This Dance?* won the New England Book Festival award for poetry and was an honorable mention/finalist at the New York and International Book Festivals.

About the Illustrators

Carrie Louise Wood is an artist across several mediums. She always strives to capture the everyday magic and connections she sees in the world in the most honest way possible. Her work was featured in the New York Times, exhibits in NYC and her photography won Voice of the Year from BlogHer, in addition to a couple of features by Elizabeth Gilbert, author of Eat, Pray, Love. She has published three books and continues to make magical art in Kansas with her family of beautiful misfits. The (Underappreciated) Life of Humphrey Hawley is her first children's book collaboration.

Rebecca Wood is an artist, illustrator, & art teacher. She received her degree in Art & English from St. Edward's University in Austin, Texas, and studied further at Istituto Michelangelo in Florence, Italy. Her work has been in the West Austin Studio Tour, several group shows, and she co-illustrated, Compair Lapin, a book of Louisiana Creole folktales. Originally from Austin, she now lives in Northeast Kansas with her family.